For my wonderful family and families
everywhere whatever their size, shape or
idiosyncrasies may be.

First published in the UK in 2017
by New Frontier Publishing Pty Ltd
93 Harbord Street, London SW6 6PN
www.newfrontierpublishing.co.uk

ISBN: 978-0-9956255-1-8 (PB)

A CIP catalogue record for this book is available from
the British Library.

Designed by Celeste Hulme

Printed in China
10 9 8 7 6 5 4 3 2 1

Happily Ever After

The Ugly Duckling

Happily Ever After

The Ugly Duckling

Illustrated by Annie White

NEW FRONTIER PUBLISHING

A long time ago a duck sat on her nest, waiting for her eggs to hatch. The sun was shining and all the other ducks were swimming in the water.

Mother Duck wanted her eggs to hatch so she could enjoy the sunshine. She didn't have to wait for long. One by one, the eggs hatched.

Everyone admired Mother Duck's four little ducklings.

They ran around in circles. 'Quack quack quack!' they said.

Mother Duck was about to leave the nest when she noticed the largest egg of all had not hatched. She sighed and sat back down for a little while longer.

But when the last egg hatched the duckling was not at all like her other pretty little ducklings. He was large and grey – quite the ugliest duckling Mother Duck had ever seen.

'Honk honk!' said the large grey duckling.

The rabbits were scared of the ugly duckling.

The hens laughed at the strange noise.

The cows chased him around the paddocks.

The next day Mother Duck took her five ducklings down to the pond. Her beautiful ducklings swam around, but her ugly duckling was left alone at the edge of the water.

'You don't look like us,' said the four
little ducklings.

The ugly duckling looked at his face
in the pond. One big fat tear fell
onto the grass.

He was indeed a very ugly duckling.

When the four little ducklings turned their backs and swam away with Mother Duck, the ugly duckling walked away.

He found a nest of birds and cuddled up with them. But when they all began to sing, he was scolded for being out of tune.

Everybody hates me, thought the ugly duckling.

A big fierce dog appeared, but when he saw
how ugly the duckling was he hurried away.

The ugly duckling wandered back to the pond.
He sat down sadly.

As he looked out across the pond, four baby swans appeared. 'Do you want to play with us?' they asked.

Well, the ugly duckling was so happy!

He dived and ducked in the water with his new friends.

'Mummy, Mummy,' called the swans. 'Come and meet our new friend. He's a duckling.'

When the ugly duckling looked up he saw the most beautiful creature he had ever seen.

'Why, you are not a duckling at all!' said the beautiful creature.

'You are a swan.'

The ugly duckling looked in the pond. He could see he was growing into a beautiful swan.

He lived happily ever after with his new family.